Where's our dinner?

Written by Gillian Liu
Illustrated by Jane Green

Evans

Evans Brothers Limited

dinner Daddy boy girl baby

Everyone was very hungry.
They all sat down to eat.

 friend  Mummy  Grandad  Grandma dog

But something was wrong.

The dinner had gone.

dinner Daddy boy girl baby

Where could it be?
They started to sniff and see.

friend　　Mummy　Grandad　Grandma　dog

That smells sweet.

Daddy sniffed on top of the shelf,
but no dinner.

 dinner Daddy boy  girl  baby

The boy sniffed under the chair,
but no dinner.

friend  Mummy  Grandad  Grandma  dog

The girl sniffed in the fridge,
but no dinner.

dinner　　Daddy　　boy　　　girl　　　baby

The baby sniffed behind the cot, but no dinner.

friend   Mummy   Grandad   Grandma   dog

A friend came to help and
they all went outside to hunt.

dinner Daddy boy girl baby

Mummy sniffed under the bonnet,
but no dinner.

 friend
 Mummy
 Grandad
 Grandma
 dog

Grandad sniffed in the garden,
but no dinner.

dinner Daddy boy girl baby

Grandma sniffed over the wall,
but . . . oh no . . . .

 friend  Mummy  Grandad  Grandma dog

She saw next door's dog . . .
and an empty dish.

 dinner  Daddy boy  girl baby

'Our dinner is in next door's dog!' she screamed.

 friend  Mummy  Grandad Grandma dog

So they all went to the friend's house for dinner instead.

Activities

What is each stall selling?
What do they smell like?

Can you think of other places
that have their own smells?

onion

sweets

perfume

smoke

cheese

fish

Can you find a set of things
that smell nice?

lemon

cake

rubbish

petrol

flowers

socks

Can you find a set of things
that smell horrible?

Where is the dog?

in

between

beside

behind

on

through

over

under